Trav

THE ZACH & ZOE MYSTERIES

MYSTERIES

THE HALF-COURT HERO

ALSO BY #1 BESTSELLER MIKE LUPICA

THE ZACH & ZOE MYSTERIES
MYSTERIES

THE HALF-COURT HERO

THE ZACH & ZOE MYSTERIES
THE HALF-COURT HERO

Mike Lupica

illustrated by

Chris Danger

Philomel Books

PHILOMEL BOOKS
an imprint of Penguin Random House LLC
375 Hudson Street
New York, NY 10014

Published simultaneously in the United States of America by Philomel Books and Puffin Books,
imprints of Penguin Random House LLC, 2018

Text copyright © 2018 by Mike Lupica
Illustrations copyright © 2018 by Chris Danger

LIBRARY OF CONGRESS CATALOGING-IN-PUBLICATION DATA IS AVAILABLE UPON REQUEST.
ISBN: 9780425289396

Printed in the United States of America.

1 3 5 7 9 10 8 6 4 2

Design by Maria Fazio
Text set in Fournier MT Std

For Hannah Grace Lupica
One more time now that she's off to college.
Boy oh boy. What a girl.

THE ZACH & ZOE MYSTERIES

MYSTERIES

THE HALF-COURT HERO

ONE

It was the Thursday after school ended for the summer in Middletown. The Walker twins, Zach and Zoe, would be heading off to camp the following Monday. But before camp was scheduled to start, Zach and Zoe had signed up to play in a basketball tournament for third-graders at Wesley Park.

They had come up with the idea the day before school let out. As soon as they mentioned it to a few kids in their class, word spread fast.

Soon, most of their classmates were eager to join. The twins' dad, Danny Walker, helped them organize the tournament. Zach and Zoe posted a sign-up sheet at the local community rec center that evening and quickly discovered they had enough players for eight teams!

Now, the first games were scheduled for the next day, Friday. The tournament would continue through the weekend, with the championship game set for Sunday afternoon.

Each team was split, three boys and three girls. Because Zach and Zoe's dad was their coach, the eight-year-old twins were getting to do something they hardly ever got to do in sports:

Play on the same team.

From the moment they found out, they couldn't help their excitement. "Game on!" they would say to each other whenever they got the chance.

Today, Thursday, was their last day of practice. Zach and Zoe's grandfather, Richie, planned to walk them to Wesley Park after breakfast. Danny Walker, who was a sports reporter on TV, had to work that day, so their friend and teammate Malik Jones's father would be running practice.

Grandpa Richie had once been a basketball star himself. First in college and then in the NBA, just like his son, Danny, had been. Zach and Zoe always loved it when their dad and grandfather joked with each other about who was the better point guard. In fact, they were doing it at breakfast.

"You know I was the better passer," their dad said.

"But I was a better dribbler," Grandpa Richie said, grinning. "And the better shooter."

"They sound like us!" Zoe said as she looked at her brother.

Breakfast was a lot of fun, the way it always was when Grandpa Richie came over. He lived close by, and came for breakfast once in a while.

But now that school was out and Zach and Zoe weren't rushing to catch the bus, Grandpa Richie had come for breakfast every day that week. And every day Grandpa Richie arrived with his morning newspaper rolled up under his arm.

Zach and Zoe's mom, Tess, often said Grandpa Richie would rather skip eating his cereal in the morning than miss reading the sports section of the paper.

"I like to keep up with the news," Grandpa Richie liked to say. "Good news and bad."

The bad news at breakfast today hadn't come from the morning paper, though. It came from Zach and Zoe. They told Grandpa Richie the same thing they'd told their parents the night before. When they showed up at the Wesley Park basketball court earlier that week, the rims were missing nets.

Grandpa Richie looked up from his newspaper, and said, "Something like that doesn't just affect the two of you. It might affect a hundred kids this summer."

"Maybe even more," Zach and Zoe's dad said.

"That court needs more than new nets," their mom said. "But I was at a meeting for the town board just yesterday. They told me there's nothing in the budget for improvements. All their money is going toward building an addition to the community rec center."

"Well," Grandpa Richie said, "somebody ought to do something. A lot has changed in the world since I was the twins' age. But a good basketball court still matters."

After breakfast, Zach, Zoe, and Grandpa Richie left the house and headed toward the park.

Grandpa Richie finally stopped talking about the court as he and the twins walked through the big archway at the entrance to Wesley Park. He said it was time to change the subject to something happier:

Basketball.

"I know you two get a kick out of listening to me and your dad argue about who was the better player when we were young," Grandpa Richie said. "But I've never asked which one of you is the better point guard."

Without hesitating, and without knowing what the other twin would do, Zach pointed at Zoe at the exact same moment she pointed at him.

The twins smiled at each other. They saw Grandpa Richie smile, too. He always seemed to be smiling when he was with them.

"Who really was the better point guard, you or Dad?" Zach asked.

"He was," Grandpa Richie said. "But don't tell him I said so."

"You know what we should do," Zoe said. "When our tournament is over, we should have a game of two-on-two in our driveway. Zach, you can play with Grandpa Richie against Dad and me."

"That would be awesome!" Zach said.

"Awesomer than awesome!" Zoe said.

Then Zoe turned and nodded at her brother, and the two of them gave each other their special high five. The one where they spun around, bumped hips and elbows, then jumped up and slapped palms.

"We didn't jump around that way when I was young," Grandpa Richie said. "I really am getting old."

Zach and Zoe giggled the way they always did when their grandfather talked about how old he was. They just thought it was funny because he was actually younger than most of the grandparents they knew.

"But holding a basketball in my hands still makes me feel young," he said.

Grandpa Richie was carrying Zach and Zoe's basketball on his hip. Suddenly, he started dribbling it, first with his right hand, then with his left. Then he bounced it through his legs and caught it from behind with his right hand without looking. Next, he flipped it over his head and caught it. Finally, he spun it on the index finger of his right hand.

"You're as quick as lightning!" Zoe said.

"As a matter of fact," Grandpa Richie said, "that's what my teammates used to say about me."

Then he stopped in his tracks. Zach and Zoe saw him staring up ahead at the basketball court.

"Hey," he said, "check out those baskets!"

He was smiling again. And when Zach and Zoe saw what he meant, they did, too.

The baskets on both ends of the court now had new white nets hanging from them.

"Where did those come from?" Zoe said.

"Maybe somebody just decided to do something nice for us," Zach answered.

"Or . . ." Zoe said, "maybe we've got a mystery on our hands!"

"They're just nets," Zach said. "It's probably not much of a mystery."

"It's still *mysterious*," Zoe said, her face lighting up. "Which makes it a mystery. We need to find out who did this."

Here we go again, Zach thought.

TWO

Grandpa Richie said he could only watch practice for a few minutes. He had his own weekly basketball game that morning at the rec center.

"Any advice for us before you leave?" Zoe asked.

"If you're open, shoot," he said. "If somebody else is open, pass the ball and let them shoot. Most of all, have fun."

"That's exactly what Dad always tells us," Zach said.

Grandpa Richie winked. "Where do you think he got it from?" Then he said goodbye to the twins and walked out of the park.

The other members of their team were already warming up on the court. Malik and his dad were there. So were Mateo Salazar and Lily Holmes and Kari Stuart. Everybody was excited about the new nets.

"Mom's right," Zoe said. "This court does need a lot more than nets."

As he checked out the court, Zach could see that the lines needed painting. In fact, the whole court looked like it could use a new coat of paint. Zoe said the benches looked like they might fall apart if somebody tried to sit on them.

"That's only if you're willing to risk the splinters," Kari said.

"But it's still a basketball court," Zach said.

"And we do have a big game on it tomorrow," Zoe said, and shrugged.

"And we finally get to be teammates," Zach said, excited.

"We need to do what Mom always tells us to do," said Zoe.

"Focus on the positives," Zach finished for her.

Once everyone had warmed up, Malik's dad suggested a game of three-on-three. He split them into two teams. Zach, Mateo, and Lily were on one team. Zoe, Kari, and Malik— their tallest player—were on the other. They decided the first team to ten baskets would win.

It turned into a really good, even game. The two teams traded baskets the whole time until the score was tied 9–9. Zach's team had the ball. He passed to Mateo over on the left side, and Mateo broke for the basket as soon as Zach did. It was Zach and Zoe's favorite play, one their dad said was as old as the game of basketball itself:

The Give-and-Go.

Zoe expected her brother would make that move as soon as he gave up the ball. They practiced it at home all the time with their dad. It's when you pass the ball to a teammate while you get yourself open. Then your teammate throws the ball back to you to shoot. This time, Zach managed to get past his sister. Malik tried to switch over and cover him as soon as Zach received Mateo's bounce pass. But he was a step too late. Zach was wide open now, and he easily banked the ball off the backboard. It swished through the new net and won the practice game for his team.

It was Malik who realized the ball had gone bouncing away, toward the bench closest to them. He jogged after it so they could hand it over to the next team to practice.

But all of a sudden, Malik stumbled in a hole in front of the bench and fell forward. He was going just fast enough that he wasn't able to stop himself in time. They all watched as Malik went crashing into the bench. He scraped the back of his hand on a jagged wooden slat jutting out.

Everyone ran toward Malik when they heard him cry out in pain. His dad got to him first. Malik's hand was bleeding, but he said the cut wasn't that big a deal. His dad cleaned it off with some water, rubbed first-aid cream on it, then covered the cut with a Band-Aid. Malik insisted if the game hadn't just ended, he would have been able to keep playing.

He was even able to joke about his injury.

"I didn't just lose to you guys," Malik said to Zach. "I lost to a bench, too!

But Malik's dad was clearly angry as he stared down at the bench. There were sharp, jagged edges, but one of the slats where you'd

normally sit was missing, too. He walked down the court and saw that the bench at the other end wasn't much better.

"This is unacceptable," he said. "I guess I didn't notice yesterday what kind of shape this court is really in. Somebody should at least do something about these benches."

At that point, Malik's mom showed up. When she found out what had happened to her son, she was just as angry as her husband.

"Something must be done about this court," she said, shaking her head. "At least the nets have been replaced."

"Maybe the court has a guardian angel who hung the nets," Zach wondered aloud. "But if that's the case, they have more work to do."

Zoe looked deep in thought. "That's right," she said. "And it could be anybody."

THREE

At dinner that night, Zach and Zoe told their parents about what happened to Malik. Grandpa Richie, who was also at the dinner table, had already heard the story after picking up Zach and Zoe from practice.

"Sometimes," Grandpa Richie said, "I feel as if they haven't made any real improvements to those courts since I was a boy."

"There's only so much money in the budget," Zach and Zoe's mom said.

Grandpa Richie frowned. "But parks are important to kids, especially in the summer."

"Nobody on the town board would disagree," Tess Walker said. "But they also feel the rec center is important to the community year round."

"I stopped by and looked at the court on the way home from work," Danny Walker said. "It's perfectly fine to play on. But Dad's right. Everything over there just looks really run-down."

"It's not right," Grandpa Richie said. "I spent half my summers on that court when I was Zach and Zoe's age."

"Same," said Danny, nodding in agreement.

Then they stopped talking about the court and shifted to a better topic: the basketball tournament.

Zach and Zoe knew both their parents cared about all sports. But basketball was the sport their dad loved most. Above all, he loved teaching Zach and Zoe everything he knew about the game.

"I can't tell you how excited I am to coach you two," Danny said.

"We all know that, dear," their mom said, smiling.

"Is it that obvious?"

"Pretty much, Dad," Zach said, and they all laughed.

After everyone helped clear the table, and Grandpa Richie went home, Zach and Zoe decided to go for a walk. It would only be a short one, as usual. Halfway up the block and back, with their parents watching from the front porch. Zach and Zoe knew how much their mom loved this time of year. During the summer, Tess loved to come outside in the evening, when the fireflies started to appear in their yard.

Zach and Zoe enjoyed those summer nights as much as their mom. But they loved their walks even better. They never got tired of being together—because, in addition to being brother and sister, they were also best friends.

They did some of their best thinking on walks like these. And tonight Zach could tell Zoe had something on her mind. He could always tell. Watching her face, Zach imagined Zoe having a whole conversation inside her head before saying anything out loud.

"What if Mom and Dad put up the new nets and are keeping it a secret?" Zoe wondered.

"You could be right," Zach said. "One of their favorite things is surprising people with presents. And we both know they're really good at holding on to secrets."

"That's true. But what I can't figure out is why they wouldn't tell us. We've already got the new nets," Zoe said.

"It's a mystery," Zach said, and winked at his sister.

They walked up the sidewalk as far as they usually did. If they went any farther, their parents wouldn't be able to see them. Then they turned back for home.

"But you know, it could be almost anybody in town who put up those nets," Zach said.

"I know that," Zoe said. "But I've just got a feeling it's somebody who has something to do with our team."

"One of those feelings you get," Zach said.

"Hey, you know how often those feelings turn out to be right," she reminded him.

"Do I ever," Zach said.

They started up their front walk and saw their parents smile and wave at them from the porch.

"So who do you think put those nets up?" Zach asked.

"I don't know," Zoe said.

He waited, knowing what his sister was going to say next. On this one, you didn't have to be a mind reader.

"At least not yet," she added.

FOUR

When they arrived at the court at Wesley Park the next morning, there were new benches.

No more jagged edges. The missing slats had been replaced. Everything looked brand-new.

The wood on the benches now looked so polished, it was as if somebody had brought it straight from Wade's to the park. Wade's was the only hardware and lumber store in Middletown.

"Whoa. The wood is so shiny, I can see my reflection in it!" Zach exclaimed.

"See," Zoe said. "Told you we have a mystery on our hands."

"We sure do," Zach said. "I don't think a professional carpenter could have done any better."

"Maybe it's what Mom calls an 'omen' for our team," Zoe said. "Like it's a sign that everything is going to go great for us this weekend."

Each tournament game would be played in eight-minute quarters. They placed a small scoreboard on a table on the sideline near half-court, not so far from where Malik had stumbled and fallen the day before.

Their team was called the Warriors. It wasn't because of the Golden State Warriors from the NBA. It was in honor of Danny Walker's old travel team, the one he'd played on when he was twelve. It was the team that won the national championship of travel basketball for kids his age.

Calling the team the Warriors had been Zach and Zoe's idea. Their dad always told them he had enough of his own sports memories.

Now he was more interested in the ones they were making.

For their first game, they were playing against the Wizards. Just like Zach and Zoe, the guards on the Wizards—David Morton and Sarah Winslow—were the best players on their team.

But as they all warmed up with some practice shots, Zoe still couldn't stop thinking about the new benches.

"First the nets," she said. "Now the benches. I want to know who our basketball guardian angel is more than ever."

"So do I," Zach said. "But what I really want to do right now is beat the Wizards."

"I'm able to concentrate on two things at once," Zoe said.

Zach grinned at his sister. "I've noticed!"

Right before the game was about to start, Zach ran over to Grandpa Richie, who was seated at the end of the new bench. Zach noticed a Band-Aid on his finger but wasn't surprised. Every time their grandpa played a pickup game at the rec center, he always came back with some kind of bump or bruise.

"Okay, Grandpa, what happened this time?" Zach said, pointing at the Band-Aid.

Grandpa Richie looked over and shrugged. "Wasn't paying attention to what I was doing," he said.

Zach and Zoe knew their grandfather always joked about how clumsy he was getting in his old age. Sometimes he called himself Mr. Clumsy.

"So what's your advice today?" Zach said.

"Same as always," Grandpa Richie said. "Hit the open man or be the open man."

"Can I do both on the same play?" Zach asked.

"Only if you're lucky," Grandpa Richie said, and patted Zach on the shoulder. "Now go get your pre-game instructions from Coach Dad."

That's what Zach and Zoe called him: Coach Dad. The last piece of advice Coach Dad gave Zach and Zoe before the game started was this:

"Keep moving yourselves and keep moving the ball. The more space you can fill on the court, the better chance you have to fill the basket."

After the huddle, Zach, Zoe, and their teammates ran out onto the court and the game began.

The game went on for the next half hour. By the fourth quarter, the score was 18–16. The Warriors were losing by one basket. Sarah Winslow had just snuck in behind Mateo and stolen the ball from him. She drove the length of the court for an easy layup to give her team the two-point lead.

Zach looked over at his dad, who didn't seem bothered by what had happened at all. He

just smiled at Zach and Zoe and waved them up the court. It was his way of telling them to just continue playing. Zach and Zoe couldn't tell who was having more fun: their dad or the players.

Now Zoe was the one bringing the ball up the court for the Warriors. As Zach ran past her he whispered, "Give-and-Go."

Zoe nodded.

She dribbled to her right as she crossed half-court, then threw the ball to Zach over near the sideline. As soon as she did, she took off for the basket, catching Sarah by surprise. Zach threw her a perfect bounce pass, right in stride. Now his sister was the one making an easy layup.

The game was tied 18–18.

With less than a minute to go, the scoreboard showed 20–20. The Wizards' David Morton missed a short jump shot and Mateo got the rebound. Now there were only twelve short seconds left in the game. If the Warriors could score here, they would move on to the second round and play another game on Saturday. If not, they'd be eliminated from the tournament.

So they were playing to keep playing.

Danny Walker called a time-out. When the players huddled around him, he said, "What could be better than this? We've got the last shot in a tie game."

"Wouldn't making the last shot be even better?" Zoe offered.

Her dad patted her on the shoulder. "My daughter's a genius," he said.

The play he gave them wasn't a Give-and-Go. It was more like a Fake-and-Go. This time he wanted Zach to fake a pass to Zoe and then drive to the basket himself.

It's exactly what he did. David fell for the fake, just as Zach hoped he would. Zach drove hard to the basket, finally hitting the ball softly off the backboard and through the net. His shot won the game for the Warriors, 22–20, just as the buzzer sounded from the clock.

Their dad had taught them to always show good sportsmanship, win or lose. So the Warriors quickly got in line to shake hands with the Wizards.

"Good call on the Fake-and-Go," Zach said to his dad.

"Only because you made the play," his dad said. "Never forget that it's a players' game."

Then he put out his hand, palm up. Zach slapped his dad a quick low five. When he looked around for his twin sister, he saw her kneeling near the Warriors' bench, holding something in her hands: a newspaper.

Zach walked over to where she was kneeling, and Zoe showed him the paper. He noticed right away that it wasn't the whole paper.

"Somebody left a sports section," she said.

"And you think this is important . . . why?" Zach asked.

"Maybe the person who fixed up these benches accidentally left it behind," Zoe said.

"Is it today's paper?" Zach asked, curious.

Zoe shook her head. "Yesterday's," she answered.

"Great," Zach said, grinning at his sister. "No problem. Now all we have to do is find the one person in the whole town missing a sports section."

"It doesn't have to be the whole town, silly," Zoe said. "It's somebody who comes to this court. And who wants to make the court better for us."

"It would figure that it's yesterday's paper," Zach said. "Because whoever fixed up these benches had to do it sometime at night. Otherwise, somebody would have seen them."

"Grandpa Richie loves his sports section," Zoe said.

Zach couldn't help himself. He laughed. "You think Mr. Clumsy fixed these benches?" he said. "On what planet?"

They talked a little more and decided that whoever was fixing up the court obviously didn't want any credit for it.

"Maybe it was Malik's parents," Zoe said. "They were pretty upset about the benches yesterday. Or maybe it really is our parents. They may have wanted to do something nice for us without anybody knowing it was them."

"All I know is that the mystery of our basketball court keeps getting bigger," Zach said.

"At least we have our first clue," Zoe said.

"A win and a clue," Zach said. "That's a good day."

"No," his sister corrected him. "That's a great day."

FIVE

When Zach and Zoe got home, they looked in the drawer where their mom kept old newspapers. She stored them there until it was time to bundle them up every week for recycling.

"We need to see if the sports section is missing from our paper," Zoe said.

"If it is, then we might have more than a suspect," Zach said.

Zoe nodded. "We might have our guardian angel."

Zach could see the excitement on his sister's face. But just as quickly, it disappeared. Because the sports section from their paper wasn't gone. So they knew the one they'd found under the park bench didn't belong to them.

When Tess came into the kitchen and saw them with yesterday's paper spread out on the counter, she asked what they were doing. Zoe explained about the sports section they'd found under the new bench.

"We just wanted to eliminate you as a 'suspect,'" Zach said.

But he put air quotes around "suspect" to let her know he was joking.

"Well, it's nice that you both think I'd go to those lengths to be your guardian angel," their mom said.

"We know you, Mom," Zach said. "You love our town, you love basketball, and you love our family."

Their dad walked into the room then, only

hearing the last part of the conversation. He laughed and said, "But not in that order, I hope!"

"What about Malik's parents?" their mom said. "I don't know of two parents from your grade any nicer than they are."

"Even nicer than you and Dad?" Zoe said.

"Nobody's that nice," Zach said.

"Your mom's right," their dad said. "Mr. and Mrs. Jones seem like just the kind of people who would do something like this."

"So you might as well put them on your list of suspects," their mom said.

"We don't need more suspects," Zoe said. "We need more clues."

"But look on the bright side," Zach said. "We usually find them."

After dinner, Zach and Zoe went to Zoe's room, where they'd left the sports section they'd found at the park. Zoe was staring at it, searching for a clue.

"I keep thinking we might have missed something," she said, her eyes glued to the paper.

Zach reached over and opened the part of yesterday's paper sitting between them on the floor.

"I know I missed something," he said. "I forgot to check the baseball box scores yesterday."

Zach loved looking at the box scores in the paper to see how his favorite players had done the day before. But when he opened the newspaper now, he noticed something.

The page with the box scores was missing. As soon as he pointed it out to Zoe, she was on her way back downstairs. When she came back up, she was holding their copy of the sports section from yesterday's *Middletown Dispatch*. This one did have the page with the box scores on it.

"Check this out," Zoe said.

Zach did and grinned. "Will Hanley got two hits yesterday!" he said.

Will Hanley was Zach's favorite Major League Baseball player. Their last mystery had involved a baseball he'd autographed for Zach.

"Not the box scores, silly," his sister said. "Look at what's next to them."

Right next to the box scores was an ad for Wade's Lumber and Hardware and a coupon that offered a discount on your next purchase at the store.

"Since this page was missing from the sports section we found at the park," Zoe said, "that could mean the person who left behind that part of the paper used the coupon."

"To buy new slats to fix a couple of benches," Zach finished the thought for her. It was something that happened a lot between the twins.

"I think we need Mom or Dad to take us over to Wade's before our game tomorrow," Zoe said. "I'll bet they'll know if somebody used a coupon like that."

"Maybe they could even find out what that person used their coupon to buy," Zach said. "And who that person is."

"And maybe what we've found," Zoe said, "is our best clue yet."

Somebody who loved basketball in their town had a secret. Now Zach and Zoe just had to find out who it was.

SIX

Zach and Zoe's semifinal game against the Bulls was scheduled for 11:30 on Saturday morning. Wade's opened at nine o'clock, which left them plenty of time to go there before they had to be at the park. That way they could do some investigating about the coupon.

Zoe thought somebody at the store might know who had come in on Thursday afternoon. She hoped they'd remember if that person bought wooden slats to fix a bench.

As they were preparing to leave the house, Zach said, "Maybe there's even some kind of record that shows if somebody used a coupon."

They looked over and saw their mom smiling at them.

"Are you sure the two of you are only eight years old?" she said. "You always seem a lot older to me."

"We get our curiosity about stuff from you," Zoe said, beaming.

"Hey," their dad said, coming down the stairs, "what about me?"

"We get our stubbornness from you," Zach said.

Their dad looked at their mom. "I'm going to take that as a compliment," he said.

"Sure," their mom said, kissing him on the cheek. "Go with that."

Their dad said he actually needed to stop at Wade's himself. He wanted to buy some fencing to put next to the driveway where Zach and

Zoe played basketball. A fence would keep the ball from rolling into the bushes.

So he drove them over to the lumber and hardware store a few minutes after nine o'clock. Zach and Zoe went looking for Ralph, the store manager. Their dad headed over to the section in the back where they sold wood fencing.

Zach and Zoe had been at Wade's plenty of times before with their parents. So they knew Ralph, and he knew them. Ralph was a tall, kind guy with a beard who'd worked at the store for as long as Zach and Zoe could remember.

"Well, if it isn't my friends the Walker twins," Ralph said when he saw them. "How can I help you?"

"Hi, Ralph," Zoe started, then got straight to it. "Do you remember anybody coming into the store to buy wooden slats? It would have been in the past couple of days."

"I was actually out with a bad cold the last few days," he responded. "But give me a few minutes to do some checking. You know I'd do anything for the Walkers." With that, Ralph turned and headed back into the stock room behind the register.

In the meantime, Zach and Zoe wandered over to where their dad was browsing for different kinds of fencing. He said being at Wade's on a Saturday morning brought back memories of when Grandpa Richie used to bring him here as a kid.

After about ten minutes, Ralph came walking back to them. He held a small piece of paper in his hand.

"It turns out somebody was in here the day before yesterday to buy the kind of slats you're talking about. Some paint, too," Ralph said.

"Paint?" Zoe said to her brother. She could see he was just as confused as she was.

"Who bought all that stuff?" Zach said to Ralph.

"Unfortunately," Ralph said, "there's no name attached to the receipt because they paid cash."

"Can you tell if they used a coupon?" Zoe asked.

Ralph looked down. "Since the price is lower than it usually would be, I'd say they probably did."

Zach and Zoe looked at each other. "Yes!" Zoe said, pumping her fist.

"Would anybody here remember who might have bought the slats?" Zach said.

Ralph looked down at the receipt again. "From the time stamp on this, it would probably have been one of the kids I hired for the summer, Mark. But he's away for the weekend with his family. He'll be back on Monday, though."

"No worries," Danny Walker said. "You've helped us plenty already."

Both Zach and Zoe politely thanked Ralph for his help. But they were having trouble hiding their disappointment. They'd both been so sure they could solve the mystery today, before their game.

By then, their dad had decided on the fencing he needed and was ready to pay for it. After he did, they started walking toward the exit when Zoe turned and said, "Wait!"

Then she ran back to ask Ralph one more question.

"What was all that about?" their dad asked when she came back.

"He said there was a time stamp on that receipt," Zoe said. "I asked him to check. It was about a half hour after our practice the other day. Which means not too long after Malik fell into the bench and scratched his hand."

"So maybe it was Malik's parents after all," Zach said. "Remember, they were really upset after he got hurt. And Dad did say they're the type of people who would do something like this."

"But why wouldn't they just admit they'd fixed up the court?" Zach said.

"Because," Zoe said, "maybe they're like Mom and Dad. You know they're always telling us a good deed is its own reward."

"But you still want to find out who did it, right?" their dad said.

Zach and Zoe looked at him and nodded.

"No surprise there," he said.

But it wasn't nearly as big a surprise as the one waiting for them when they got to the park for their game.

SEVEN

The entire court had been painted.

The lines were a bright white. The three-point line had a fresh coat of red paint. Everything about the court looked brand-new. Just like the benches had yesterday, and the nets the day before.

"How did this happen?" Zoe said, staring at the court.

"And when did it happen?" Zach added.

"I'll tell you one thing," their dad said.

"Whoever's looking out for this court must be doing it in the middle of the night. If not, the paint wouldn't be dry by now."

"If that's true," said Zoe, "then how could they have seen what they were doing in the dark?"

"I know the park is lit up after sundown," their dad said. "We used to play at night when I was in high school. But I don't know when the lights turn off."

"We don't know, either, Dad. We've never been to the park late at night," Zach said. "But now we know for sure the receipt Ralph found had to belong to our guardian angel. Because whoever bought the slats also bought paint."

"I'll tell you something else," Zoe said. "Our guardian angel must have had helpers, because I can't believe one person painted this whole court by themselves."

"It's like the more we find out, the more questions we have!" Zach said, throwing his hands up.

"I still think our answer might be Malik's parents," Zoe said. "I'd like to know where they went after practice that day."

"We can ask them when they get here for the game," Zach said.

But right then, Zoe's face fell. She shook her head sadly as she pointed toward the park entrance. Zach looked over and saw Malik walking up to the court. But his parents weren't with him. Instead, his babysitter walked him to the park. When Zach and Zoe asked Malik where his parents were, he told them they were picking up his older sister from the airport. They probably wouldn't even make it back in time for the game.

"Did you need them for something?" Malik asked.

"It can wait," Zoe said. "Don't worry about it."

Zach and Zoe's dad came walking over then.

"How about for the next hour or so," he said, "we all just worry about lighting up this court."

Zach and Zoe agreed. They ran onto the court to start warming up with the rest of their team. They knew they had their work cut out for them against the Bulls. Two of Zach's teammates from his rec league, Dylan Barnes and Tommy Bellino, were playing. Tommy had been the tallest player on their team last season. But he was also a great shooter from the outside. Dylan played point guard, so he'd be guarding Zach today and Zach would be guarding him.

Emily Curley, one of Zoe's teammates from her rec league, was also playing for the Bulls. Zoe would be guarding her in today's game. Right before they started, Zoe looked over to where her mom was sitting with Grandpa Richie and a few men she didn't recognize. She ran up to Zach.

"Are those friends of Grandpa Richie's?" she asked him.

"I think those are some of the men he

plays basketball with at the rec center," Zach answered.

"Well," Zoe said, "if it makes our cheering section bigger, that's fine with me."

After almost twenty minutes of play, the buzzer went off to mark the end of the second quarter. The Bulls were ahead, 18–8, mostly because Tommy Bellino had made every one of his shots in the first half. By the end of the third quarter, the Warriors were still losing by eight points, 22–14. If they didn't start playing better, and fast, they wouldn't be playing in the final on Sunday afternoon. Instead, they'd be watching it from the sidelines.

Before Zach and Zoe took the court for the fourth quarter, their dad pulled them both aside.

"Even though the Bulls are winning, I think they've started playing a little defensively. It's like they're worried about losing their lead," Danny Walker said. "And I think they're getting tired."

"So what's our game plan?" Zoe asked.

"You chase them harder than ever," their dad said. "And make them chase you."

"Sounds like a plan to me, Coach Dad," Zach said.

With just over a minute left, the Warriors were still down by six points. But on the next two plays, Lily scored for the Warriors, and then Malik made a steal from Tommy and scored. Now they were only losing 26–24.

Next, Zach stole the ball from Dylan Barnes and passed to Mateo, who was running down the court. Mateo caught the ball and drove in for a layup.

The game was tied, 26–26.

With fifteen seconds left, Emily missed an outside shot that would have put the Bulls back ahead. Zoe got the rebound. Then Coach Dad called a time-out.

"So, what's our play?" Zach asked as they huddled by the sideline.

Their dad grinned, and said, "You tell me."

"But you're the coach," Zoe said.

"Yeah," their dad said. "But what am I always telling you?"

"It's a players' game," Zach said.

"We've been talking about surprises," Zoe said. "So let's surprise them. Kari hasn't taken a shot since the first half. Let's have her take the game-winning shot."

"But how do I get open?" Kari asked.

"You go stand over on the left side," Zoe said. "Zach will be on the right side with the ball. You call for it. Loudly. As soon as you do, cut for the basket, and my brother will hit you with a pass."

"You sound pretty sure about this," Kari said.

"I know my brother," she said.

Zoe made the inbounds pass to Zach. He dribbled to his right. As soon as he did, Kari yelled really loudly that she was open. Lilliana

Martinez, the Bulls player covering Kari, turned her head. When Kari saw that, she took off. Zach threw a crosscourt pass to Kari that she caught in stride. By the time her layup was through the net, the Warriors were through to the finals.

After the handshake line, Zach and Zoe stood with their dad at midcourt.

"We're right where we want to be," Zach said.

"All we need to do now is win the championship game and find out who's been fixing up the court," Zoe said

Their dad shook his head.

"You two don't give up, do you?" he said.

"It's like you always say, Dad: we never quit. Whether it's school, sports, or mysteries," Zoe reminded him.

"Well, I've got to admit," their dad said, "you've got me there."

EIGHT

After dinner that night, Zach and Zoe's parents came into the living room, where they were watching TV.

"Let me ask you guys a question," Tess Walker said, taking a seat between them on the couch. "Even if you do find out who did all these nice things for you and your friends—will it make any difference?"

"I know what you're saying, Mom," Zoe said. "But you know how much I like to figure things out."

"Same," Zach said.

"And it's one of about two million things I love about you both," their mom said.

"But let me ask you another question," their dad said. "As happy as you'll be if you do find out, what if it makes the person fixing the court even happier keeping themselves a secret?"

"We've talked about that," Zach said. "What we really want to do is thank that person. We think it's even more important than solving the mystery."

Then Zoe said, "Mom, don't you always tell us there's nothing more precious than an act of kindness?"

"I do," their mom said. "So does your dad."

"Well," Zoe said, "Zach and I want to reward one act of kindness with one of our own."

"Sounds like a pretty great idea to me," their mom said.

"Now, I've got another idea," Danny Walker said. "How about the two of you shoot a few hoops until it's time to go to bed?"

And that's just what Zach and Zoe did. They played a game of one-on-one while their parents cheered them on from the front porch. Zach and Zoe looked over at them and realized this was another kind of reward: all four of them being together as a family.

NINE

Sunday was the Warriors' big championship game against the Rockets. That morning, Zach and Zoe arrived at Wesley Park to another surprise on the basketball court. Little did they know, it wouldn't be the only surprise they'd get that day.

A big yellow lightning bolt had been painted across the half-court line.

Their dad walked toward the center of the court and stared down at it. It was almost as if he were the one trying to solve the mystery. And it looked like he might have discovered another clue.

"What do you think it means, Dad?" Zoe asked.

Their dad shrugged and put his hands up, as if to say he had *no* clue.

"All I know is that somebody's really having fun now," he said.

The championship game between the Warriors and the Rockets was even more fun, the way the best competitions in sports always are. The Warriors had already played two close games in the tournament. Today was no different.

They ended up tied with the Rockets, 24–24, with thirty seconds left on the clock. The Rockets' best player, Marcus Beverly, had just missed a wide-open shot after making most of the shots he'd taken in the second half. Mateo beat everyone to the rebound, but he got so close to the baseline chasing down the ball that Zach was worried he might step out of bounds. Not wanting to take any chances, Zach quickly called time-out.

"Let's move ourselves and move the ball until it's time to take the last shot," their dad said in the huddle.

"But what's the play?" Zach asked.

"We wait until the clock hits ten seconds," Danny Walker said, "and then whoever has the ball follows Grandpa Richie's advice."

"If you're open, shoot," Zach said.

"If somebody else is open, pass the ball and let them shoot," Zoe said.

Their dad put his hand out in the middle of the huddle. Everybody on the team put a hand on top of his.

"And have fun!" Zach and Zoe shouted at the exact same moment as their dad.

From the sideline, Zoe passed the ball in to Zach, who was standing right on top of the lightning bolt. Zach passed it back to her. She passed to Malik, who gave the ball back to Zach just as the clock showed ten seconds left in the game.

Zach dribbled right. Then he drove left for the basket. Then he noticed Zoe just to the left of the free throw line. She was wide open, but she didn't call for the ball or wave for it. It didn't matter. She knew it was coming to her

the second she met Zach's eyes. It was like the twins were reading each other's minds.

Five seconds.

Four.

Zach passed the ball to his sister with two seconds left. Zoe squared up her shoulders as she faced the basket, just the way their dad and Grandpa Richie had taught them.

Then she shot the ball.

They all heard the buzzer sound right before Zoe's shot went through the net and won the Warriors the championship.

Now it was time to celebrate. All six Warriors players jumped up and down on the lightning bolt at midcourt.

TEN

The whole Warriors team and their parents (plus Grandpa Richie) gathered in Zach and Zoe's backyard a couple of hours after the game for a team barbecue and victory celebration.

The championship trophy had already been presented to them at Wesley Park. But Zach and Zoe's dad said he wanted to wait to award the MVP trophy at the party, along with trophies for all the Warriors players.

Their dad handled the grilling and stood by

the barbecue with a few of the parents. Their mom made a huge salad. Some of the other guests brought side dishes and desserts. Everybody was in a wonderful mood. It seemed they weren't just celebrating their tournament win, but also the beginning of summer.

Zach was going over the ending of the game with Malik and Mateo when he noticed Zoe standing by herself. He walked over to her.

"What's wrong?" he asked. "You just made the kind of shot you remember forever."

"You know what's wrong," she said, frowning.

Zach nodded. He knew she meant they hadn't solved the mystery of the basketball court.

"But we won the championship," he said to his sister, trying to make her feel better. Right now, he only wanted her to feel great about her game-winning shot.

"We still didn't solve the mystery," she said. "I was hoping Malik's parents would turn out to be our guardian angels. But I asked them about it as soon as the game was over. They promised it wasn't them."

"So that means it must have been one of the other parents," Zach said.

"But who?" Zoe said. "I keep thinking it was somebody who saw Malik cut his hand on the bench. There were a bunch of parents watching the practice game."

"I don't know," Zach said. "It made perfect sense for it to be Malik's parents. Especially when we found the time stamp on the receipt at Wade's. Whoever bought the slats and paint did it right after our practice game ended."

"But then who put up the new nets?" Zoe wondered.

Right then, Grandpa Richie came walking over. "How about the two of you show me that fancy high five?" he said.

That seemed to make Zoe feel better. So she and Zach spun and bumped hips and elbows and jumped. When they came down, Zoe noticed the yellow stain on Grandpa Richie's old shoes.

"You've already got mustard on you?" Zoe teased.

He grinned. "Are you saying Mr. Clumsy strikes again?"

Then their dad came over and told Zach and Zoe the team trophies were in a box in the basement. He asked if they'd go get them while he went to get the MVP trophy out of the trunk of his car.

Zach and Zoe hardly ever went into their dad's basement office. It was more of a trophy room than an office, really. Many of Danny's old awards were down there. There were photographs all over the place. Some hung on the walls, and some were stacked in piles in the corner. But by now, the twins knew how much their dad preferred living in the present, not the past.

Zach quickly grabbed the small box of trophies off his dad's desk. He turned and headed out the door, carefully making his way back upstairs.

But Zoe stayed behind. She stared at a small, framed photograph hidden in a corner behind a file cabinet. She'd never noticed the picture before. It was of three boys in matching basketball jerseys. Zoe thought the boy in the middle was their dad, at first. He didn't look much older

than she and Zach were. The boy was holding a basketball on his hip, smiling like he'd just won a big game. And his jersey had a lightning bolt on the front. The same lightning bolt that had been painted on the court at Wesley Park.

At that moment, a lightning bolt went off in Zoe's brain. She had just solved the mystery of the basketball court.

Zoe carefully took the photograph off the wall and made her way upstairs. She smiled to herself. Making the winning shot for her team felt pretty great. But solving the mystery felt even better. Suddenly, a lot of things made sense to Zoe, and her day was complete.

Well, almost.

ELEVEN

Back in the yard, Zach and Zoe's dad asked everyone to form a big circle around him. He then proceeded to hand out trophies to all six Warriors players. For each player, he pointed out something they did to help the team win. Not just in the championship game, but all weekend.

Then it was time for the presentation of the MVP award. The MVP was decided by the other seven coaches in the tournament through a vote. All the coaches had attended the championship game.

"It was unanimous," Danny Walker said. "All the coaches agreed the MVP award should go to the player who made the winning shot— Zoe Walker!"

A great cheer went up in the Walkers' backyard.

"Just what this family needs: another basketball trophy," said Grandpa Richie, and he winked at Zach, who was standing beside him.

Zoe walked up to her dad, and Zach noticed she was holding something behind her back in her left hand. He couldn't see what it was, but he knew Zoe was up to something. Their dad handed Zoe the MVP trophy, which she held easily in her right hand.

But then Zoe turned to everyone, and said, "I tried to be as good a player today as I could possibly be. But I don't deserve this trophy as much as the person who spent the last few days making our basketball court as good as it could possibly be."

She smiled and showed everybody the picture

in her hands: the picture of a boy wearing a jersey with a lightning bolt on the front.

Zoe smiled at Grandpa Richie. "For that act of kindness, I would like to present this trophy to my grandfather."

Now a much bigger cheer exploded in the backyard. It was so loud, Zach and Zoe thought people all over town could hear it. Everyone turned and looked at Grandpa Richie, who smiled and shrugged.

"Busted," he said.

TWELVE

Later that afternoon, after the party was over and all the guests had gone home, Zach and Zoe, their parents, and Grandpa Richie sat together in the backyard. They went over some of the highlights from the game and laughed about catching Grandpa Richie in his act of kindness.

Grandpa Richie kept saying he didn't know what the big deal was.

"I didn't do it to hear a few more cheers," he said. "I've heard enough of them in my life. It was the right thing to do. And you're supposed to do the right thing when you have a chance."

He told them that originally, he was only planning to buy new nets for the court. "On the way home from my game at the rec center Wednesday afternoon, I passed through the park and noticed the baskets. Figured it'd be easy enough to replace the nets." But then he heard Zach and Zoe talking about the court at breakfast on Thursday, and realized the court needed more than that. When Zach and Zoe told him about Malik's accident after he picked them up from practice, he decided to repair the benches, too. Luckily, on the same day, he'd noticed the coupon for Wade's in the newspaper.

"It didn't hurt to know I could save a few dollars," he said. "We old guys have to watch how we spend our money."

Zach and Zoe giggled the way they always did when he called himself old. Their dad came over and patted Grandpa Richie on the back.

"I know you keep saying that, Dad," he said. "But when I watch you play basketball with your friends at the rec center, you sure don't look old to me."

"My friends at the rec center are part of the story, too," Grandpa Richie said. "In fact, I was just getting to them."

Everyone turned back to Grandpa Richie to hear the rest of the story.

"I was afraid I might get caught when I remembered I'd left behind my sports section after fixing up the benches," he said. "But I was so focused on going home to get a Band-Aid for my finger after that old bench gave me a nasty splinter."

"Mr. Clumsy," Zach said.

Grandpa Richie went on. "At Wade's, I figured I might as well pick up a can of paint or two while I was at it. It's probably been years since that court was painted. I just knew I had to do it fast, before your championship game."

Zoe wanted to know how he'd pulled that one off, especially so late at night. Grandpa Richie explained how some of his basketball friends from the rec center offered to help and even brought lights.

"And what about the lightning bolt?" Zach asked.

"I couldn't help myself," he said, "even if I was afraid your dad might figure things out."

"I hadn't looked at that old picture in so long," their dad said. "Even I'd forgotten his youth league team was called the Bolts."

"I was a little clumsy doing that, too, as it turned out," Grandpa Richie said. "I didn't notice the yellow paint on my shoe until Zoe did."

"Wait," Zoe said, a little confused. "You said it was mustard."

"No," he said, pointing to Zoe. "*You* said it was mustard."

"You faked us out!" Zach exclaimed.

"I've still got a few moves left," said Grandpa Richie.

It was getting late, and Grandpa Richie said it was time for him to go. But Zach and Zoe wouldn't let him leave. At least not yet. There was still one more game to play.

"It's for a different kind of championship," Zoe said. "The championship of our driveway. An all-Walker showdown."

As planned, the game would be Zoe and her dad against Zach and Grandpa Richie. The first team to reach seven baskets would win.

It figured there would be one last close game for the Walker family that weekend. Zoe and her dad were winning 6–5, but then Grandpa Richie made a long shot from the outside to tie the game at 6–6.

"Nice shot, Grandpa!" Zach said.

"You do still have a few moves left, Grandpa," Zoe said.

They were playing winners' outs, which meant you kept the ball if you scored. So Grandpa Richie and Zach would now have their chance to win.

But before Zach or his grandfather went for the winning shot, Grandpa Richie put on a little show with the basketball.

He dribbled with both hands, then bounced the ball between his legs. Then he dribbled behind his back with the ball, not just once but twice, before putting the ball between his legs again. It was all so much fun to watch that their dad actually started laughing.

Even Zoe turned her head to watch. And when she did, Zach made his move.

He took off for the basket. Without hesitating, and without even looking in Zach's direction, Grandpa Richie whipped him a perfect pass. As soon as Zach caught the ball, it was his turn to sink a game-winning shot.

Zach ran straight toward Grandpa Richie as soon as his shot went through the net, ready to give him a high five. But his grandfather put out a hand to stop him. Then he smiled and spun the way Zach and Zoe did for their

special high five. Zach spun, too. They bumped elbows and hips, and Zach jumped up to high-five his grandfather.

In that moment, Grandpa Richie didn't look old at all. He looked young—as young as the boy in the picture with the lightning bolt on his jersey.

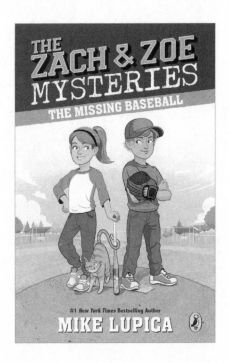

READY FOR ANOTHER MYSTERY?

LOOK FOR:

THE ZACH & ZOE MYSTERIES

THE FOOTBALL FIASCO